Enid Blyton's™
ENCHANTED LAND

The
Grabbit Gnomes

Hippo

Mollie and Peter have a big secret. The chair in their garden playroom is a Wishing Chair! Sometimes, it grows wings and whisks the children off on wonderful adventures! Mollie and Peter can't watch the chair all the time, but Jigs can. Jigs is their pixie friend who lives in the playroom. Whenever the chair grows its wings, Jigs runs to fetch them . . .

Scholastic Children's Books,
Commonwealth House, 1-19 New Oxford Street,
London WC1A 1NU, UK
a division of Scholastic Ltd

London ~ New York ~ Toronto ~ Sydney ~ Auckland

First published in the UK by Hippo, an imprint of Scholastic Ltd, 1998

Text Copyright © Abbey Communications Ltd, 1998
© Copyright in original stories and characters Enid Blyton Limited
Enid Blyton ™ Enid Blyton's signature is a registered Trade Mark of Enid Blyton Limited
Audio-visual series © Copyright Abbey Home Entertainment Limited, 1998
Licensed by PolyGram Licensing International.
Script adaptation by Pat Posner
Story consultant – Gillian Baverstock

ISBN 0 590 11347 X

Printed in Belgium

10 9 8 7 6 5 4 3 2 1

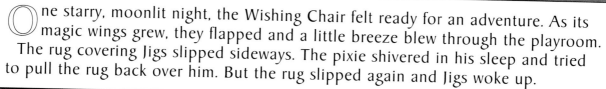

One starry, moonlit night, the Wishing Chair felt ready for an adventure. As its magic wings grew, they flapped and a little breeze blew through the playroom. The rug covering Jigs slipped sideways. The pixie shivered in his sleep and tried to pull the rug back over him. But the rug slipped again and Jigs woke up.

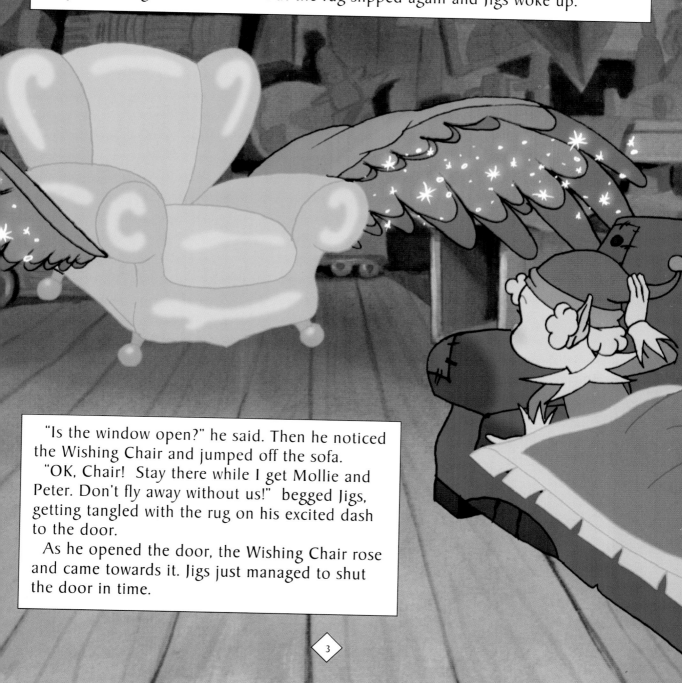

"Is the window open?" he said. Then he noticed the Wishing Chair and jumped off the sofa.

"OK, Chair! Stay there while I get Mollie and Peter. Don't fly away without us!" begged Jigs, getting tangled with the rug on his excited dash to the door.

As he opened the door, the Wishing Chair rose and came towards it. Jigs just managed to shut the door in time.

He ran across the garden and climbed up a pear tree. He reached out and tapped on Peter's bedroom window. "Come on, Peter! Wake up!" Jigs called softly.

Suddenly the window was flung open. Jigs lost his balance and found himself hanging upside-down from the branch.

"Psst! Down here!" said Jigs, when Peter and Mollie looked out. "The Wishing Chair has grown its wings!"

"Great!" whispered Peter. "We'll get dressed."

"Just put your dressing-gowns on!" Jigs said impatiently. "And hurry up!"

The three of them climbed down the tree and dashed to the playroom. Jigs opened the door and a couple of minutes later, the Wishing Chair was flying swiftly up into the night sky!

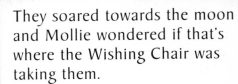

They soared towards the moon and Mollie wondered if that's where the Wishing Chair was taking them.

But the chair dipped down and flew beneath the stars.

At last dawn broke and the chair flew downwards to a strange wood and a village of toadstools.

"Oh, no!" cried Jigs "The Grabbit Gnomes live here. They grab **everything**!"

"They'd better not grab our Wishing Chair!" said Peter as the chair landed by a large tree.

"Let's explore!" Mollie said excitedly, tugging Peter towards the village.

"Be careful!" Jigs called. "The minute the Grabbit Gnomes see you, they'll start grabbing! Grabbing anything and everything!" he added, pulling a piece of string from his magic pocket. As he pulled, the string turned into a length of rope that coiled round his feet.

Meanwhile, Mollie and Peter were walking round the village. There was nobody about, but Mollie noticed that one of the toadstool tables, outside a toadstool house, was set for breakfast.

"Let's see what they're having," said Peter moving towards it.

All at once, there came the sound of angry voices: "Robbers!" "Burglars!" "Thieves!" It was the Grabbit Gnomes – watching and shouting from different doorways and windows!

"How dare you come here grabbing things!" yelled one gnome, running out. "That's our job!"

Then, more gnomes arrived. They made a circle around Mollie and Peter and started chanting: "Robbers! Thieves! Robbers!"

Suddenly, Jigs came running up. He pushed his way in between two of the Grabbit Gnomes. A moment later, the gnomes were tumbling to the ground, one by one, like dominoes! "They aren't robbers! They're children! They're visitors!" shouted Jigs.

"How did you get here?" one of the gnomes asked Mollie.

"We came on our Wishing Chair!" she replied proudly.

"Ooooooooh! A wishing chair!" cried the gnomes excitedly. "We've always wanted a wishing chair!"

They jumped up and danced around, their little grabbing hands grabbing at the air. "Grabbit! Grabbit! Grab the Wishing Chair!" they chanted. Then, they dashed towards the wood.

Jigs tried to stop them, but one of the gnomes grabbed him and passed him around as if he were the parcel in 'pass the parcel'! The last Grabbit Gnome dropped him on the ground in front of Mollie and Peter.

By the time Mollie, Peter and Jigs reached the tree where they'd left the Wishing Chair, the Grabbit Gnomes had climbed on to it.

"Chair, take us to our treasure cave!" ordered one of the gnomes.

"We can't get home if you take our chair!" shouted Peter.

But the Wishing Chair was already rising into the air!

Then Mollie noticed something hanging from the chair. Jigs had used the string-that-had-turned-into-a-rope to tie the Wishing Chair to the tree! The Wishing Chair couldn't fly away, and it was too high in the air for the Grabbit Gnomes to jump off!

"Jigs, you're brilliant!" said Mollie. "And now you've grabbed them, we can go exploring!"

"You two go," said Jigs. "But only for half an hour. I'll stay here and look after the Wishing Chair."

When Peter and Mollie arrived back in Toadstool Village, three toddler Grabbit Gnomes invited them to sit down and share their breakfast.

The toddlers offered their guests cereal and toast, then grabbed the food away again! One toddler poured Peter a mug of lemonade. His little brother grabbed it and poured it all over Peter. Then the other brother grabbed the lemonade bottle and splashed it all over Mollie.

Just then, Mother and Father Grabbit Gnome came out of the toadstool house. "The cheeky Grabbit toddlers have made your dressing-gowns dirty." Mother Gnome said. "Come inside and we'll wash them for you."

While Mother and Father washed their dressing-gowns, Peter and Mollie sat on toadstools in the kitchen, licking lovely ice-creams Mother Grabbit Gnome had given them.

But, oh, dear! Mother and Father Grabbit Gnome liked the dressing-gowns so much they decided to grab them!
  They grabbed the ice-creams back, too, and ran outside, leaving Peter and Mollie locked in!

"We've got to get out of here!" said Mollie. "Jigs is waiting for us!"

"I know that!" said Peter crossly, jumping up. "And we **must** get our dressing-gowns back!" said Mollie.

"I know that too!" said Peter. He noticed the curtains moving gently. Peter pulled the curtain aside and found the window wasn't properly closed. "There's no catch on this window," he cried.

"I expect one of the gnomes grabbed it!" said Mollie.

"But it means we can get out!" Peter laughed.

In the garden, Mother and Father Grabbit Gnome were pegging the dressing-gowns on to the clothes line.

"Grabbit! Grabbit!" shouted one of the toddlers, tugging the washing basket away.

"Come here, you cheeky little Grabbit!" shouted Mother Gnome.

"Bring that washing back at once!" yelled Father Gnome, as he followed them.

While Mother and Father Gnome were busy chasing the first toddler, his brothers ran to the clothes line. "Grabbit! Grabbit!" they shouted gleefully and they grabbed the dressing-gowns.

Giggling loudly, the toddler gnomes raced off down the path.

"Grabbit! Grabbit!" yelled Peter and Mollie, jumping out from behind two bushes. They grabbed their dressing-gowns from the toddler gnomes.

"Back to Jigs!" said Peter. "This way."

They hurried down the path and before long they came to a large toadstool. Mollie heard laughter and dashed over to peep in one of the toadstool's windows.
"It's a school!" she called. "And there's a Teacher Gnome, teaching pupils how to grab things!"

20

"Grabbit! Grabbit!" a voice shouted as Mother and Father Grabbit Gnome grabbed Peter and Mollie from behind. "Now you're grabbed, we're taking you to our treasure cave!" said Father and the two Grabbit Gnomes carried the children towards the wood.

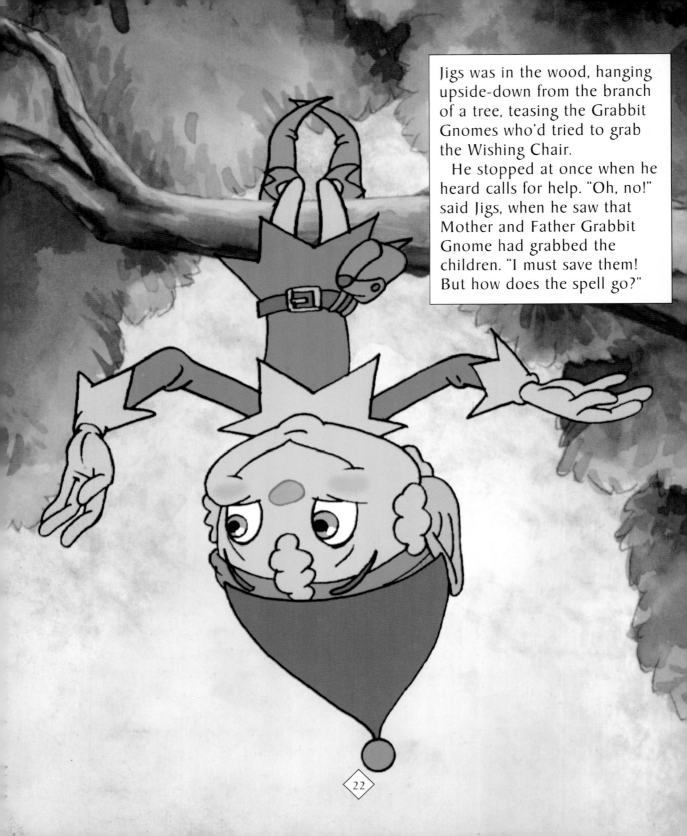

Jigs was in the wood, hanging upside-down from the branch of a tree, teasing the Grabbit Gnomes who'd tried to grab the Wishing Chair.

He stopped at once when he heard calls for help. "Oh, no!" said Jigs, when he saw that Mother and Father Grabbit Gnome had grabbed the children. "I must save them! But how does the spell go?"

Jigs clicked his fingers at some ivy climbing up the tree next to him. Two strands unravelled. They raced towards Jigs and grabbed his ankles. Jigs hadn't meant that to happen! He clicked his fingers again. And . . . the strands of ivy uncoiled from Jigs and wriggled downwards just in time to grab Mother and Father Grabbit Gnome around their ankles!

   They were lifted up into the air with cries of horror and Mollie and Peter found themselves looping the loop. The children landed neatly on the ground beside Jigs, who'd just jumped down from the branch.

"Let's get away before I have to think up more magic!" said Jigs, pointing to the rope attached to the Wishing Chair.

The three of them gave a sharp tug on the rope. The chair shot downwards. The Grabbit Gnomes fell off and Mollie, Peter and Jigs leapt on.

"They'll pull us down!" cried Mollie as the Grabbits tried to grab the rope.

But clever Jigs had used a magic knot. The rope twirled loose and fell to the ground. As the gnomes fought over the rope, the Wishing Chair flew up and away.

Mollie, Peter and Jigs were on their way home, just in time for breakfast.